Leicestershire
Libraries & Information Service

SAUVAIN, P.   621.042J
Carrying energy
£6.90
13.5.88 110

Charges are payable on books overdue at public libraries. This book
is due for return by the last date shown but if not required by
another reader may be renewed — ask at the library, telephone
or write quoting the last date and the details shown above.

CARRYING ENERGY

PHILIP SAUVAIN

Editorial planning
Deborah Tyler

M
MACMILLAN

First published 1987

Published by
MACMILLAN EDUCATION LTD
Houndmills, Basingstoke, Hampshire RG21 2XS
and London
Companies and representatives
throughout the world

Designed and produced by BLA Publishing Limited,
East Grinstead, Sussex, England.

Also in LONDON · HONG KONG · TAIPEI · SINGAPORE · NEW YORK

A Ling Kee Company

Illustrations by Fiona Fordyce, Val Sangster/Linden Artists,
Clive Spong/Linden Artists, Brian Watson/Linden Artists
Colour origination by Planway Ltd
Printed in Hong Kong

British Library Cataloguing in Publication Data

Sauvain, Philip
    Carrying energy. — (Exploring energy). —
(Macmillan world library).
    1. Fuel — Transportation — Juvenile
literature
    I. Title   II. Series
    621.042   HE199.5.F8

ISBN 0-333-44177-X
ISBN 0-333-44180-X Series

Photographic credits

t = top b = bottom l = left r = right

5*t* Chris Fairclough Picture Library; 5*b* The Hutchison Library; 7 ZEFA; 8*t* The Hutchison Library; 8*b* ZEFA; 9*t* Dick Clarke/Seaphot; 9*b* Shell; 11*l* Hugh Jones/Seaphot; 11*r* British Petroleum; 13, 14, 15*t* Shell; 15*b* The Hutchison Library; 17*t* ZEFA; 17*b* Shell; 18 Science Photo Library; 21 Mansell Collection; 27 Science Photo Library; 28, 29 Central Electricity Generating Board; 31 David George/Seaphot; 33 ZEFA; 34, 35 Central Electricity Generating Board; 37 Chris Fairclough Picture Library; 38 Science Photo Library; 39 ZEFA; 42 Science Photo Library; 43*t* Her Majesty's Stationery Office

Note to the reader
In this book there are some words in the text which are printed in **bold** type. This shows that the word is listed in the glossary on page 46. The glossary gives a brief explanation of words which may be new to you.

Contents

Introduction

There would be no life in the world without **energy.** People, animals, plants, machines and cars all use energy. This energy comes from different sources, such as oil, coal and sunshine.

The word 'energy' comes from a Greek word for 'work'. The word has a special meaning in science. Energy is something that can do work. It can make our bodies move. Energy can make something change from one form into another. When a piece of wood burns, its **chemical energy** turns into heat and light. Energy is useful because one kind of energy can be changed into another kind of energy, or moved from place to place.

Energy for people and machines

We use energy when we walk, stand or sit. We even use energy when we sleep. We get our energy from food. Our bodies burn up food to release energy. Cars and machines get their energy from **fuel,** such as oil, gas or coal. The world was very different before people learned how to use fuel. Today, we burn fuels to heat our homes and to make trains, cars, planes and ships move. We cannot make energy but we have learnt how to use the energy in fuels. Also, we have learnt to turn some forms of energy into **electricity.** Electricity makes lights, machines and tools work.

▼ The Sun's energy reaches all parts of the world as sunshine. Coal, oil and natural gas are carried by ship and train, or by road and pipeline to the people who use this energy. Wires carry electricity from power stations to homes and factories.

Types of energy

Energy is never used up. It moves in a chain from one form to another. Energy that is stored in fuel and food, or even in the still water of a lake, is called **potential energy**. This means the energy is waiting to be used. When energy is in use, it moves. It may be transferred as heat. Water may flow from a lake as a stream or waterfall. Electricity flows along wires. Anything which is moving has **kinetic energy**. So energy in use is called kinetic energy.

▼ Many people have machines to do work for them. In some parts of the world, there is no fuel for machines. People have to use their own muscles to dig the soil and grow food. Sometimes they have animals to help them in the fields or to carry heavy loads.

▼ People need fuel to work. Our fuel comes from food. The food comes from plants and animals which owe their existence to the Sun. When we eat hamburgers, our bodies use the energy stored in the meat and the bun. We also use energy such as electricity to cook our food and light the shops where we buy food.

Where energy comes from

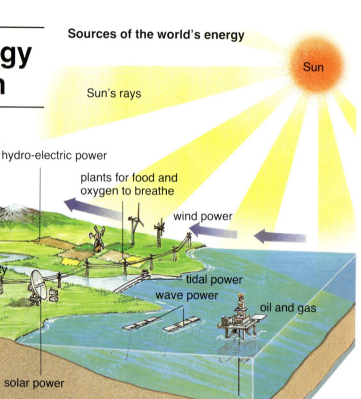

Sources of the world's energy

Sun

Sun's rays

clouds

rain

wood

hydro-electric power

plants for food and oxygen to breathe

wind power

coal

electricity

nuclear power

tidal power

wave power

oil and gas

solar power

heat from the inside of the Earth

Fuel is stored energy. When **petrol** burns, oxygen in the air releases the stored energy. This makes the car move. Food is also stored energy. When people and animals breathe, oxygen in the air releases the stored energy in the food. Muscles need this energy to move.

Energy passes in a chain from the Sun to the fuel and the food we use. The Sun's energy is called **radiant energy**. Heat and light from the Sun travel as rays which spread out in all directions. Sunshine makes plants and trees grow. The leaves use sunshine to take a gas from the air. The roots take water and goodness from the soil. Trees and plants turn all these things into food. They use the Sun's energy to grow new wood and new leaves and fruit. When a tree is chopped down and when fruit is picked, energy is stored in the wood or fruit. The Sun's energy is released when the wood burns or fruit is eaten. This transfer of energy is called the **energy cycle**.

Storing the Sun's energy

Over 300 million years ago, trees and plants stored the Sun's energy in the same way. When they died, their remains lay in the water that covered the Earth. Mud and sand slowly covered the remains of these plants and the remains of tiny sea creatures. The weight of more mud and sand pressed these layers of remains into rocks. After millions of years, the bodies of the tiny creatures turned into oil and natural gas. Dead trees turned into seams of coal. Oil, natural gas and coal are called **fossil fuels** because they are the remains of living things.

▶ You can see electrical energy in a flash of lightning. Think of the power in a rushing river filled to the brim with rain. You can feel the energy of the Sun when it shines on your face and feel the force of the wind during a storm. Energy is all about us. We have to find the best ways of using it.

The Sun is the source of the other forms of energy as well. The Sun's heat makes winds blow. Windmills can use this wind power to make electricity. Also, winds make waves on the sea. Wave power, too, can be used to make electricity. The heat of the Sun makes water **evaporate** to form clouds. The clouds cool and water falls again as rain. The rain flows into rivers. Some rivers are used to make **hydro-electricity**.

We will always have rain, wind and sunshine. They are **renewable** sources of energy. However much of this type of energy we use, there will always be more. Other renewable sources of energy include the tides and waves.

There is also heat inside the Earth. We can use this heat. It is called **geothermal power**.

The world's energy

Oil, coal and natural gas are **non-renewable** sources of energy. It took millions of years to make them. Once they are used up, they are gone for good. Renewable and non-renewable sources of energy are not evenly spread across the world. Coal is found in most of the largest countries but a lot of oil and gas are found in remote places where few people live. Some countries have more sunshine or stronger winds and faster rivers than others.

Most sources of renewable energy, such as wind and water power, can only be used on the spot. Energy is needed where people live. Coal, gas and oil can be carried to different parts of the world. It is important to find the best and cheapest way to carry energy to people who want to use it.

Oil and gas by pipeline

Oil and gas cannot be used as soon as they come out of the ground. **Crude oil** is only useful when it has been turned into other products, like petrol. Natural gas must be treated at a **gas plant**. Many of the world's biggest oil and gasfields are in the middle of deserts or jungles, or under the sea. First of all, the oil and gas must be carried to a **refinery** or a gas plant. Then the products are carried to the people who can use them. If the oil or gasfield is very large, it is worth laying a pipeline. Once the pipeline is laid, oil and gas flow through it easily, even in bad weather.

Pipelines on land

A pipeline may be laid for hundreds of kilometres from the oil or gasfield to the nearest port. Pumping stations keep the oil or gas moving through the pipes. Shorter pipelines carry oil and gas from refineries to towns and factories. Some pipelines carry different types of oil in one pipe. The pipes are very big. In remote places, the pipeline can be laid over the ground.

▲ It is not always easy to take a pipeline overland. If a lot of people live nearby, the pipeline must be buried in the ground. Also, it is safer and does not look ugly. First, mechanical diggers make a trench. Then trucks bring the heavy pipes to the site. Welders join the pipes together, and cranes lower the sections into the trench. The welders join the sections of pipe together to make the pipeline. The soil is put back and farmers can use the land above the pipeline again.

▶ In very cold places above the Arctic Circle, oil pipelines cannot be buried. The heat of the oil would melt the frozen earth and cause problems. The Trans-Alaskan pipeline carries oil for 1300 km from the oilfield at Prudhoe Bay to the nearest ice-free port of Valdez. The pipeline is high enough for migrating caribou to pass underneath.

Pipelines at sea

It is harder to lay pipes under the sea. Lengths of pipe are welded together on board a ship. The ship is called a lay-barge. Cranes lower the pipeline on to the sea bed from the back of the barge. The pipe is covered in concrete to keep it on the sea bed. In some busy seas, the pipe has to be buried in the sea bed to keep it out of the way of ships.

▶ Here, divers are at work on a pipeline on the sea bed.

▼ The first part of this gas pipeline was welded into 300 m sections on land. Mechanical diggers lower it into a trench near the shore. A barge pulls the pipeline out to sea. Then a lay-barge adds more lengths in the deeper water, until the pipeline reaches the gasfield.

Oil and gas by tanker

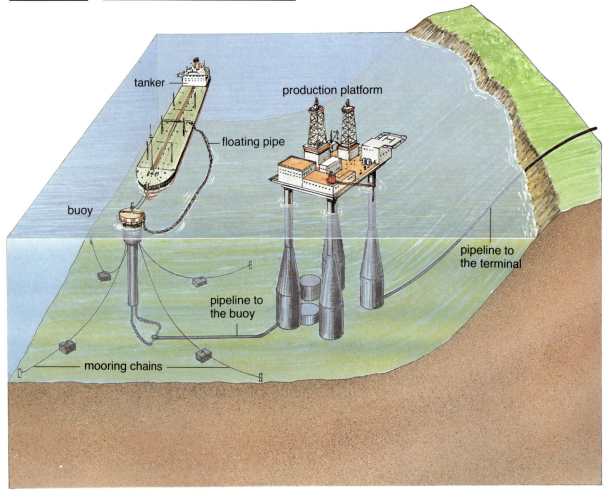

tanker

floating pipe

production platform

buoy

pipeline to the terminal

pipeline to the buoy

mooring chains

Some pipelines carry crude oil and natural gas to the nearest port. From there, the crude oil and natural gas is sent to a refinery by ship. Half the cargo, or **freight**, carried by the world's ships is oil or natural gas. **Tankers** can carry oil and gas over very long distances. They load their cargo in the Middle East and take it to Japan, Europe or North and South America. A pipeline is fixed between two places. A ship can travel to any port. When a ship is loaded, the oil company can decide who to send the cargo to. The company will sell it to the people who pay the highest price.

The first oil tanker was built over 100 years ago. It carried oil in wooden barrels. Oil companies still measure their oil in barrels, although it is now carried in huge cargo tanks. Very large tankers, called supertankers, carry as much as 200 000 tonnes or over a million barrels of oil on each journey. Today supertankers can carry as much as 500 000 tonnes of oil.

◄ Tankers and pipelines can carry oil and natural gas from oilfields under the sea. Tankers tie up about two kilometres from an oil platform. They carry over 700 000 barrels of oil on each journey. The tankers cannot load or unload in bad weather. Pipelines take oil and gas to the shore from the biggest oilfields.

Unloading at sea

Supertankers need very deep water to load and unload their cargo. The water in many ports is not deep enough for such huge ships. In the Gulf in the Middle East, small offshore islands have been built in deep water where supertankers can tie up. The world's largest port is Rotterdam in the Netherlands. Special structures for supertankers stretch five kilometres out into the North Sea. At many ports, tankers tie up at a **single buoy mooring**, or SBM. Each buoy is firmly fixed to the sea bed in deep water offshore. Floating pipes link the ship's cargo tanks to the buoy. Oil is pumped out of the ship and carried by a pipeline in the sea bed from the buoy to storage tanks on the shore.

Gas by tanker

Shipping gas is a bigger problem than shipping oil. Gas takes up about 1000 times more space than oil. A spark can easily make gas explode. Many oilfields used to burn off the gas which is often found with oil. It was too difficult to carry the gas to the people who could use it. Then scientists found out how to cool natural gas to −160°C so the gas turns into a liquid. Liquefied natural gas, or LNG, takes up much less space. It can be carried by special ships. The tanks on the ship keep the LNG cold.

▲ Special ships carry gas to places far from gasfields.

◄ A tanker ties up to a single buoy mooring off the coast of Nigeria. The longer the tanker's journey takes, the more the oil costs. The tanker must load and unload very quickly.

Refining oil

The first oil refineries were built near oilfields. At the refineries, crude oil was made into useful products. Small ships carried these products all over the world. Some countries bought mainly petrol. Other countries wanted lots of oil products for their industries. Today, people all over the world use oil for many different things. It is cheaper for a very large ship to carry crude oil to the places where most people live. There people make the products they want in their own oil refineries.

▼ Crude oil is changed into oil products in an oil refinery.

A refinery at work

To understand what happens to oil in a refinery, you need to know what oil is made of. The tiniest part of everything in the world is called an **atom**. There are two different types of atoms in crude oil. They are atoms of **hydrogen** and atoms of **carbon**. Atoms do not stay on their own. They join together in many different ways to make **molecules**. Hydrogen and carbon join to make molecules called **hydrocarbons**. Crude oil is a mixture of thousands of different hydrocarbons.

At a refinery, crude oil is heated to separate the hydrocarbons into different groups. Each group is called a **fraction**. All the hydrocarbons in a fraction have the same number of carbon atoms. The crude oil is heated to 350°C and pumped into a tall column called a **fractionating tower**.

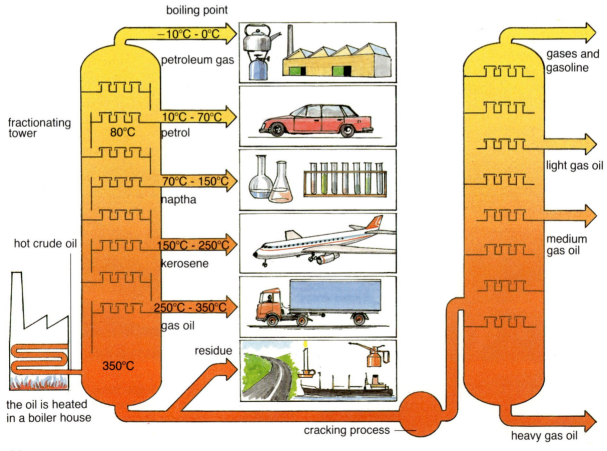

▶ Most oil refineries are by the sea, like this refinery at Moerdijk in the Netherlands. Supertankers carry oil from the oilfield to the refinery. Smaller ships, pipelines and trucks carry the products to the people who use them. You can see the place where the ships tie up in the background. Pipelines carry oil and its products from one part of the refinery to another. There may be 16 km of pipelines. The tall towers are fractionating towers.

The tower is heated from 350°C at the bottom to 80°C at the top. The hydrocarbons have different boiling points. Some fractions are still liquid at 350°C. They sink to the bottom of the tower. Other fractions boil and become a vapour. As the vapour rises through the tower, it loses heat. Fractions which are still vapour at 80°C go straight to the top. Other fractions find the level at which they cool back into liquids and are piped away.

Changing oil products

The process in the towers is only the first of many things that happen in an oil refinery. Crude oil does not separate into exactly the fractions people want. In winter, we use more heating oil but in summer more people want petrol for their cars. Oil refineries have to change their products to supply what people want to buy.

Scientists can change one oil product into another by a process called cracking. This means cracking or splitting the chains

of molecules. The molecules are made to change shape by using heat or a **catalyst**. A catalyst is a substance that makes a change take place. There are no waste products from an oil refinery. Everything is used.

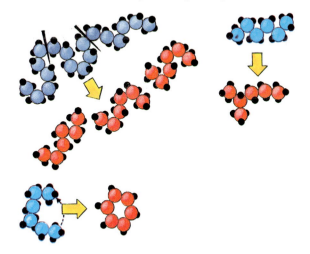

▲ Less useful oil products can be changed into more useful ones. The process changes the shape of molecules. Long chains can be shortened. Branches can be added to straight chains. Loops can be closed into a circle. Each shape is a different oil product.

Petrol by road and rail

▲ Oil products are carried very long distances in Australia by 'road train'. A road train is a line of trailers pulled by a heavy truck. This road train is carrying petrol from the refinery at Darwin to storage places, or depots, along the Stuart Highway. The Stuart Highway crosses Australia from north to south.

More petrol is used than anything else made from oil. Over 300 million cars, trucks and other motor vehicles use the world's roads. They burn a vast amount of fuel every day. Almost all of this fuel is either petrol or **diesel** oil. Diesel oil is another fuel made from oil. It is mainly used by high-powered engines in trucks, trains, ships and in some cars.

Supplying the customer

The oil refineries make different types of petrol. Each type or grade of petrol suits one type of engine more than it suits others. Different grades of petrol are needed in hot and cold countries. The weather affects the way the petrol burns.

Pipelines take petrol and other fuels direct from refineries to the largest users, such as airports and railways. Rail tank wagons and road tankers take the fuel to filling stations and pump it into underground tanks. Most motor vehicle drivers get their petrol or diesel oil from filling stations.

Out of the way places

There were no filling stations in the early days of motoring. Motorists bought petrol in cans and they carried the cans in their cars. People who live in remote places also need fuel for their vehicles. Petrol or diesel oil is delivered in cans or drums to places where only small amounts are needed. Cable cars or helicopters take it up the mountain sides. Camels carry drums of petrol through the deserts. Motor sledges carry oil for vehicles and for heating to homes in the Arctic.

Liquefied Petroleum Gas

Many trucks and buses in the United States run on liquefied petroleum gas, or LPG. LPG is the butane and propane gas which is found in both natural gas and in oil. These gases become liquid when they are under pressure. When the pressure is released, LPG turns back into a gas. LPG is easy to carry in containers and easy to store. It is used to heat buildings that are far away from pipelines. Campers use bottled LPG for cooking and lighting.

▲ Large amounts of petrol are carried by rail in special tanks. Trucks carry smaller loads to places that are not near a railway line.

▼ Car and lorry drivers must know where they can buy extra petrol during a long journey. This filling station is in the desert in Algeria in northern Africa. Road tankers bring petrol to fill the storage tanks.

Moving coal

It is not as easy to move coal as it is to move oil and gas. Coal takes up a lot of space. Also, it is heavy and dirty to handle. There is no point in mining coal if you cannot move it. The first coal mines were by the sea. Boats took the coal to the towns. There were no railways in those days.

Moving coal by train and ship

Much of the world's coal is now burned to make electricity. Some power stations have been built near coalfields. Railways are used to bring the coal direct from the coal mines nearby.

Power stations which are away from the coalfields are often built at the coast or on the banks of a river or canal. Coal barges, or special cargo ships called **bulk carriers**, tie up alongside the power station.

Coal is carried to some power stations on a 'merry-go-round' or MGR. A MGR is a train which does not stop. The railway wagons are loaded from coal storage towers at the coal mine. The train moves on to the power station. There, the track leads into a building called the **hopper house**. As the train enters the hopper house, doors on the bottom of the wagons open. The coal falls into hoppers underneath and the doors close again. The empty train circles back to the coal mine within an hour.

▼ A 'merry-go-round' loads coal at the coal mine and unloads at the power station without stopping.

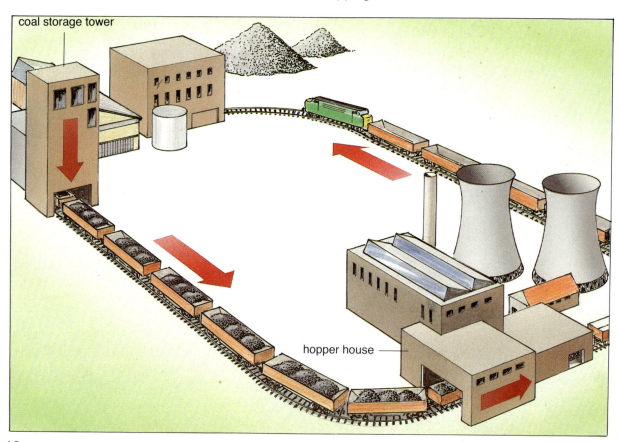

coal storage tower

hopper house

Other ways of moving coal

Conveyor belts carry coal direct to some power stations from nearby coal mines. In parts of the United States, crushed coal is mixed with water to make a liquid called **slurry**. The slurry is sent by pipeline to the customer. The Black Mesa pipeline is in the state of Arizona, in the United States. The pipeline pumps liquid coal a distance of 450 km to the neighbouring state of Nevada.

Coal is also sent by road. The truck drives on to a **weighbridge**. The load of coal is weighed with the truck. Loading and unloading is done by a machine or a conveyor belt.

▲ The Crows Nest coal plant in Canada is over 600 km from the sea. Trains carry coal from these storage towers to the coast. From there, ships take the coal to Japan.

▼ Conveyer belts load coal on to the bulk carrier *Tectus* at Port Kembla, New South Wales, Australia.

Energy all around us

An atom is the smallest part of any substance. We cannot see atoms with our eyes but scientists study them. They know that atoms have a **nucleus** in the middle. Things called **electrons** move around the nucleus. The nucleus is made up of two very small things. One is called a **neutron**. The other is called a **proton**. Atoms are held together because there is a strong attraction between electrons and protons. This is because electrons have a **negative charge**. Protons have a **positive charge**.

Opposite charges attract one another. Atoms have the same number of electrons as protons. The energy is held in the atom because the positive and negative charges balance.

Electricity

The Greeks first saw the effect of electricity over 2000 years ago. But they did not know why it happened. A Greek rubbed a stone called amber with a piece of silk. He noticed that a strange force made dust stick to the amber. Today we know that the force was **static electricity**. Rubbing some things together makes heat. The heat frees electrons from some atoms. Electrons from the cloth stuck to the amber. This extra negative charge on the amber attracted the dust. Many years later, an Englishman called William Gilbert found he could charge other things with energy, like the amber. He called this energy electricity from the Greek word 'elektron', which means amber.

▼ Most of an atom is empty space. Protons and neutrons cling together to form the nucleus. There is always the same number of protons as neutrons. Electrons travel around the nucleus, just as the Earth travels around the Sun.

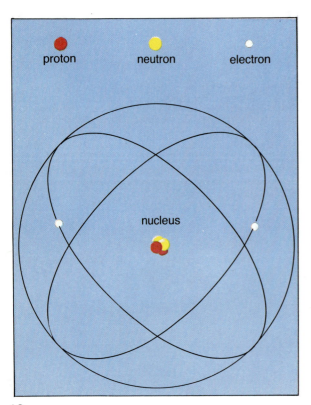

proton   neutron   electron

nucleus

▼ This is a piece of metal called tungsten, as seen through a very powerful microscope. The microscope makes the piece of metal three million times larger than its real size. The black shapes show the atoms that make up tungsten.

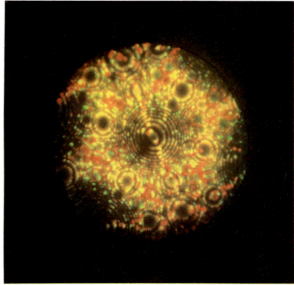

Electricity in clouds

The first person to find out about positive and negative charges was the famous American statesman called Benjamin Franklin. He lived from 1706 to 1790. He proved that lightning is electricity. Franklin showed that electricity can be divided into positive charges and negative charges. The moving air in a storm separates some of the negative charges in the atoms in the thunder cloud. These electrons are strongly attracted to positive charges on the ground. They jump the gap. This causes a giant spark of electricity or flash of lightning.

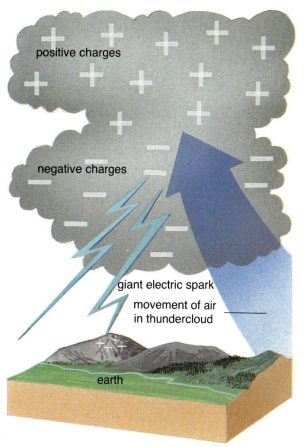

positive charges

negative charges

giant electric spark

movement of air in thundercloud

earth

▼ Benjamin Franklin risked his life when he flew a kite in a thunderstorm in 1752. He proved that a flash of lightning is a giant electric spark. Lightning charged a piece of metal on his kite with electricity. Two men who later tried to do the same thing were both killed.

Power in batteries

The charges in static electricity stay still. The word 'static' means 'not moving'. The electricity in a house is not static. When a switch is turned on, an **electric current** flows. The current makes the television or the light or any electric machine work. The current is millions of electrons moving through a wire. The electrons are strongly attracted to a positive charge at the other end of the wire. An electric current does not start on its own. A power supply makes the electrons move.

Making a current flow

A battery is a power supply. It makes electrons flow to light the bulb in a torch or play cassettes. One part of a battery has a negative charge. The other has a positive charge. When a wire is joined to both parts, it makes a **circuit**. This means

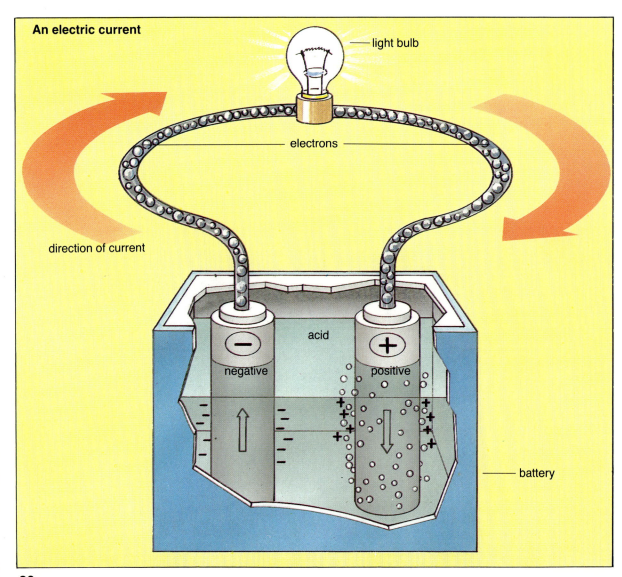

An electric current

light bulb

electrons

direction of current

acid

negative

positive

battery

electrons can move along the wire. Electrons have a negative charge so they are attracted to the positive end of the battery. They keep moving around the circuit. A switch joins the wire in a circuit. When the switch is turned off, the circuit is broken. The electrons cannot move through the wires anymore.

How a battery works

The first electric battery was made in 1800 by an Italian called Alessandro Volta. He was a famous scientist who was born at about the time that Benjamin Franklin was finding out about the electricity in lightning. Volta discovered that some metals and a liquid could act together to produce, or **generate**, electricity.

Volta's battery made electricity because electrons are released when a **chemical reaction** takes place. Electrons move from one atom to another. Volta used the chemical reactions of different metals with a liquid called **acid** to make positive and negative charges on his battery.

Electric batteries

Batteries are very useful because they make electricity that you can carry around with you. Batteries are used in torches, portable radios and recorders, watches and children's toys. These batteries do not make electricity forever. When they are used up, you throw them away and buy new ones.

There are many types of electric batteries. Some batteries can be recharged, like those in a car. A car battery starts the motor and works the lights at night. When the car is moving, the car makes electricity. This electric current flows through the battery in the opposite direction. The current makes the chemicals in the battery change back to their original state.

▼ **Alessandro Volta was the first person to make an electric current flow. The measurements of power in batteries are called volts. Here, Alessandro Volta is demonstrating how his battery works.**

Making things turn

Many people think that the wheel was the world's most important invention. It made things turn. The wheel was invented about 5000 years ago when carts were first used to carry heavy goods. About 2000 years ago, watermills and later windmills turned the first machines. Wind and water turned the mill wheels slowly but the power supply was free. Today, much of our work is done by electric motors. Electricity makes the motors turn.

Magnets

Electric motors would not work without **magnets**. The Chinese were the first people to find out that the Earth is a giant magnet. All magnets have two **poles**, known as north and south. The north pole of a magnet is attracted to the south pole of another magnet, but not to another north pole. The Chinese hung magnetic rock from their ships. It always pointed north and south. This was the first **compass**. For many years, people tried to find out more about **magnetism**, or the way magnets work.

In 1819, a Danish scientist called Hans Christian Oersted found a link between electricity and magnetism. He noticed that an electric current passing through a wire made a compass needle turn at right angles to the direction of the current. The electric current made the wire act like a magnet. In 1831, a British scientist called Michael Faraday tested a new idea. If an electric current made a magnet turn, could a turning magnet make electricity? Faraday found it could. He pushed a magnet in and out of a coil of wire. This made an electric current flow through the wire. We still use this method to make electricity today.

▼ In 1831, Michael Faraday was the first person to make electricity with a magnet and a coil of wire.

You can make a model of a windmill using the simple materials shown here. Cut the sail out of cardboard. You can make the windmill do work for you. Blow on the sail to make it lift the paperclip.

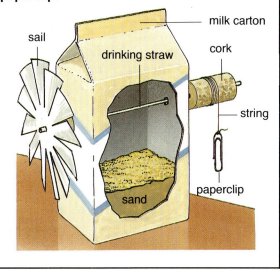

▼ **The wire loop acts like a magnet with the two poles when the electric current is switched on. It turns half a circle each time the current switches its poles from north to south or from south to north.**

Electric motors

Electric motors are used every day. There are tiny electric motors inside clocks and watches. Huge motors power electric trains.

A simple electric motor works when an electric current flows through a wire loop between the two poles of a magnet. When the electric current flows, the wire acts like a magnet. It becomes an **electromagnet** with north and south poles. If the current changes direction, the poles on the electromagnet change. The north pole becomes the south pole and the south pole becomes the north pole. The 'new' north pole of the electromagnet turns to the south pole of the magnet. The electric current then changes direction. The north pole of the electromagnet is now a south pole, so it moves on towards the north pole of the magnet. Each time the current changes direction, the magnetic forces push the electromagnet so that it swings around between the poles of the magnet. The current continues changing, and the electromagnet continues turning.

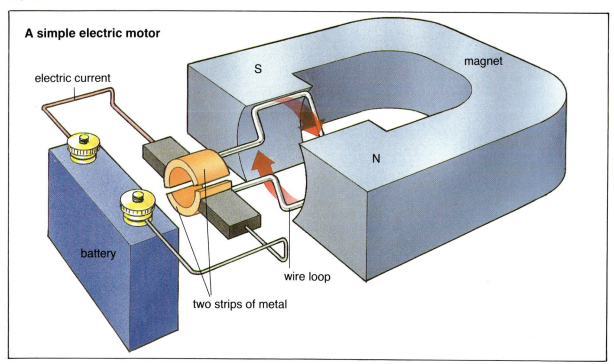

A simple electric motor

Pipelines and sea routes

Coal, oil and gas are not always found where people want to use them. Moving these sources of energy from one place to another costs money. The longer it takes, the more it costs.

China uses more coal than any other country in the world. There are a lot of coal mines in China, but there is very little oil or gas. So the Chinese use most of their coal themselves. The United States and Australia mine more coal than they need. They sell it to other countries like Japan

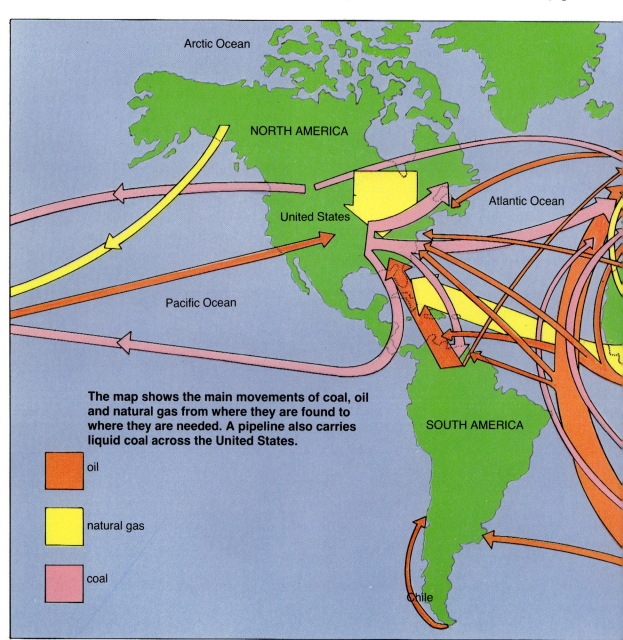

The map shows the main movements of coal, oil and natural gas from where they are found to where they are needed. A pipeline also carries liquid coal across the United States.

- oil
- natural gas
- coal

and Western Europe. Japan has very little oil and natural gas and not many coal mines. So Japan has to buy the energy needed by her many industries. Japan is a group of islands, so most coal, oil and gas comes by ship.

In North America and Europe, pipelines as well as tankers carry oil and natural gas to most people who use the oil and gas. Oil from Tierra del Fuego on the southern tip of South America goes to the big cities of Chile by ship. There are too many mountains so it is difficult to build a pipeline through them. Ships cannot be used to take oil from the Arctic oilfields. The Arctic Ocean is frozen over for most of the year. The oil is taken by pipeline to ice-free ports and then it is loaded on to ships.

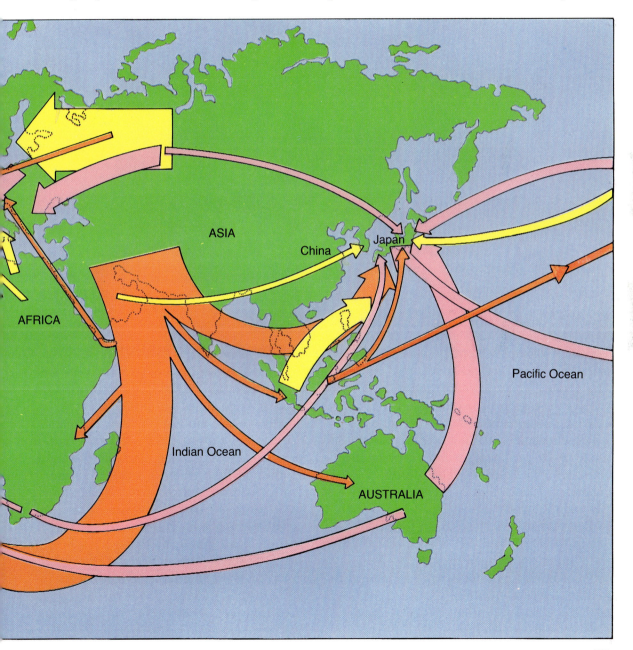

Power stations

▼ Thomas Alva Edison started the world's first public electricity supply. His power station in Pearl Street, New York, opened in 1881.

Power stations generate electricity by using the same method as Michael Faraday did. Huge electromagnets turn at high speed inside coils of wire to produce electric power. The first electric generator which could be used in a power station was made in 1871. It was made by a Belgian engineer called Zenobe Theophile Gramme. The generator worked like an electric motor in reverse.

Ten years later, the Edison Company began to supply part of New York City in the United States with electricity. At first, the six generators kept breaking down, but people saw how useful electricity could be. In 1882, Edison's system began to make electricity for street lights in London.

Inside a power station

The first power stations were very small. They only made a small amount of electricity to supply buildings nearby. Today, power stations are much bigger. One power station can supply two million people. The massive generators can light 20 million light bulbs at the same time.

Most power stations work by heating water until it turns into steam. Then, the steam turns the blades of **turbines**. A turbine is a type of motor with a wheel that turns very fast. The wheels of the turbines are connected to huge electromagnets in the generators. The generators change the **mechanical energy** of the turbines into electrical energy.

Energy for power stations

Electricity is always made from other sources of energy. Some power stations burn oil, coal or gas to make steam. A **nuclear power station** uses the energy from atoms. Atoms of a metal called uranium are split by a special process. This releases kinetic energy and heats water to make steam.

Running water and wind can also turn turbines. At hydro-electric power stations, water flows quickly down pipes to spin the blades of huge turbines. Strong winds can turn turbines but 300 large windmills would be needed to make the same amount of electricity as one power station.

The movement of tides and waves can also be used to make electricity. These renewable sources of energy cannot be moved from where they occur to where they are needed. Most sources of renewable energy are only useful for making electricity. Electricity is easy to carry to the people who use it.

▼ A nuclear power station is very clean. Just one speck of uranium fuel can generate enough electricity to boil hundreds of kettles. There are very few jobs for people to do in a nuclear power station. The people who work there wear protective clothing because the waste from nuclear power stations is very dangerous.

Carrying electricity

▼ Farmers can still plough the land underneath electricity cables. The land is not wasted but pylons carrying power lines are an ugly sight in beautiful countryside.

Power lines, or **cables**, carry electricity from the power stations to the customers. These cables are very thick wires. The wires are bound tightly together between layers of materials inside a tough casing. The cables must be able to carry electricity over long distances. Few people want to live next door to a power station. Electricity is easier to carry than coal, oil or gas.

Cables above the ground

In many countries, the power lines link up to form a giant supply system, called a **grid**. Electricity leaves the power stations on overhead cables. These cables are carried high above fields and over hills. Tall steel **pylons** hold up the cables. These towers that support the cables are sometimes called transmission towers.

Outside the towns there are often long lines of pylons criss-crossing the countryside. This is the cheapest way to carry electricity to the consumer, but there are problems. Steel pylons do not last forever. Most last about 80 years. Sometimes, pylons and cables are knocked over in bad weather, such as heavy snow, hurricanes and tornadoes.

A fault in the system that carries electricity from the power station can bring chaos. Many people rely completely on electricity, such as dairy farmers with electric milking machines, and banks and offices which do much of their business on computers. One night, in November 1965, something went wrong at the power station at Niagara Falls. Millions of people living on the east coast of Canada and the United States had no electricity for two days.

Cables underground

Pylons take up too much space in towns. Electricity has to be carried under the ground in built-up areas. The cables are buried in trenches below the surface, like pipelines. Underground cables also carry electricity near airports where pylons would be a hazard to aircraft. Cables are dug into sea beds and river beds too, so they are kept out of the way of ships and boats. It is safer to carry electricity under the ground. However, it costs 20 times more to put cables under the ground than it costs to put them up overhead.

▶ The engineers who look after overhead power lines have a difficult and dangerous job to do. Many of the worst problems occur in bad weather. The engineers have to find the faults in the line and then mend them, while perched high above the ground.

Bringing power into the home

oil tanker · OIL

storage tank

electricity cables

electricity main

J. STEVE

▲ Most homes in a town are supplied with gas from a gas pipeline in the road and with electricity from a mains cable. You cannot see them because most of the pipes and cables are buried below the road surface. They can only be seen when workers have to repair them. In some places, electricity cables are overhead. Some people have to find space to store oil, wood or gas in bottles.

Power stations have to produce electricity when people need it. Electricity cannot be stored for future use. Demand for electricity is low in the middle of a warm night. Some power stations close down then. Extra generators stand by to supply the power needed when the demand rises. This often happens in the evening when a popular television programme comes to an end. Millions of people switch on lights and cookers at the same!

Electricity and gas

Power companies sell electricity and gas. They supply the electricity or gas to their customers' homes. In most towns, cables and pipelines carry the electricity and gas under the ground. These are the mains supplies. At intervals along the cable or pipeline, thin cables and small branch pipes take electricity or gas to all the homes in the road. **Meters** measure the amount of gas and electricity used in each home. The advantage for customers is that they do not have to store the electricity or gas. Nor do they have to order it in advance.

BUILDERS

GAS

bottled gas

place to store coal

wood

coal

ain

COAL

Bottled gas, coal and oil

Not all homes around the world have cables and pipelines. Some people buy gas in containers for their cookers and heaters. These bottles are very heavy. Coal can be delivered to the door by truck. Coal is dirty and space has to be found to store the sacks of coal. Oil is brought by road tanker and pumped into a storage tank. In some places, people are only allowed to use fuels that produce little or no smoke when they burn. This is so that there is less **pollution**.

◄ People living in remote places, such as lonely farms, often make their own electricity using an oil-fired generator or windmill. This windmill supplies a farm in Malta, an island in the Mediterranean Sea.

How lights work

For some people, their only light at night comes from a fire. Over 100 years ago most of the homes in North America and Europe were lit by candles and oil lamps. They gave out a weak light which was not bright enough to read by. The lights had to be carried from room to room. These lights were a fire risk, and they were expensive. Poor people sometimes went to bed when it became dark in order to save the cost of candles. People wanted a strong, steady light which was easy to use, cheap to run, and safe in the home.

Joseph Swan and Thomas Edison

In 1860, the British scientist, Sir Joseph Swan, made an electric light bulb using a piece of carbon to give out light. This **filament** is the part of a light bulb which glows when the electric current is turned on. Before Swan's light could work properly, he had to get rid of all the air inside the bulb. Otherwise, there would still have been enough oxygen left inside the bulb to burn the filament.

The American inventor, Thomas Alva Edison, set out to solve the problem. After many attempts, he found a way to remove all the air from a glass bulb to make a **vacuum**. This meant the bulb was empty of gas. In 1879, Edison made a filament of carbon by scorching a piece of cotton thread. Then he made an electric current light up the filament. Edison's lamp burned for 40 hours. Swan also succeeded in making a vacuum bulb in the same year. Soon electric light bulbs were lighting thousands of homes in Britain and America.

▼ When the switch is pressed down to the on position, a spring is released. The contacts are pushed together. The circuit is complete and electricity can flow. Electrons flow along the wire into the glass light bulb. The electrons pass along the coil of very thin tungsten wire, called the filament. The filament becomes white hot. When the switch is pressed to the off position, the contacts separate and electricity cannot flow.

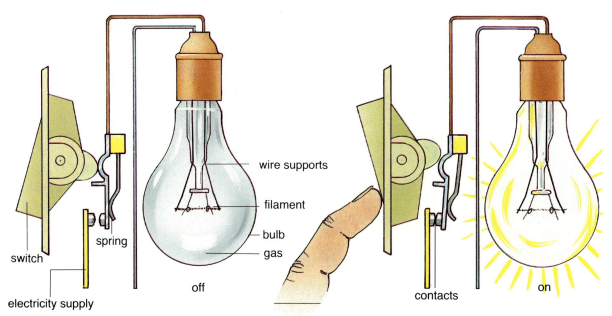

wire supports

filament

bulb

gas

switch

spring

off

electricity supply

contacts

on

► Car headlamps, street lights and millions of light bulbs light up cities like New York, in the United States, at night.

Electric light

Later inventors improved the electric light bulb. They replaced the carbon filament. Instead of making a vacuum, they filled the glass bulb with a gas called argon. Nothing can burn in argon. Electric light bulbs like these last for hundreds of hours. Many light bulbs now have a filament made from a coil of very thin **tungsten** wire. Tungsten is used because it has to get very hot before it will melt. The filament is a coil, so there is a lot of wire to light up when the current is switched on. The electrons heat up the tungsten wire until it is white hot and glows with a bright light. There is no oxygen in the bulb so the filament does not burn up and turn into ash.

Often, **fluorescent light** is used in schools, shops and offices. This is a glass tube which is painted on the inside with a substance that glows brightly when an electric current flows through the glass tube. This type of light uses less electricity than a filament bulb. Today, some light bulbs for lamps work like a fluorescent tube and do not have a filament. They can give 6000 hours of light and they do not use much electricity.

Using lights

People in the 1880s thought the first electric lamps were wonderful. People went to bed later because they could now read at night. Street lights made it safer to walk outside at night. Electric lights which could be easily carried around at night were also invented in the 1880s. A battery made the electric current which lit up a small bulb. Bicyclists also used these batteries in their bicycle lights so they could ride at night.

Thick and thin wires

▼ You can see electricity. You may have seen a spark of electricity when you switched on a light or a flash of lightning during a thunderstorm. Here engineers are carrying out tests on high voltage cables.

Metal wires are used to carry electricity because metal lets electrons flow easily. This is due to the fact that metal has a low **resistance**. Some things, like rubber, have a high resistance. Electricity does not travel well through rubber because there are not many free electrons in rubber. Some metals have an even lower resistance than others. The size of the wire makes a difference too. Thick wire has a lower resistance than thin wire. Thick wire can carry more electricity. It is like using a six lane motorway instead of a footpath.

Thin wires

The wire in the filament of a light bulb is very thin. Such thin wire heats up quickly because it has high resistance. The electrons bump into each other and jump about. They give off heat and light energy. There are very thin wires in a **fuse**. A fuse is fitted into electric machines and circuits in homes. If the wires carrying electricity around the building or to the machine get too hot, the very thin fuse wire gets even hotter. The fuse wire melts quickly and cuts off the supply of electricity.

A transformer

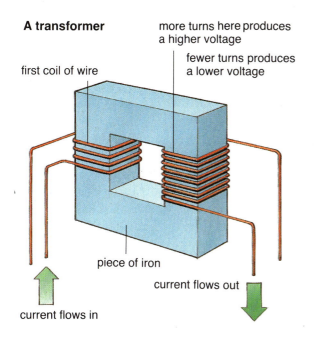

more turns here produces
a higher voltage

fewer turns produces
a lower voltage

first coil of wire

piece of iron

current flows out

current flows in

▼ A power station generates electricity at 25 000 volts. Transformers increase the current to a very high voltage, up to 400 000 volts. It is cheaper to carry a high voltage along the cables between pylons. Then the voltage is decreased at a substation like this before it is carried to shops, schools and homes.

Measuring the force

An electric current is a flow of electrons. The force of a current is measured in volts. The number of volts describes the pressure, or **voltage**, that makes the electrons move along the wire. Power stations generate electricity at a very high voltage. The voltage is increased even more by **transformers** before the current is carried away from the power station. A transformer is a piece of iron in the shape of a square with two coils of wire around it. An electric current flows through the first coil and makes it an electromagnet. The iron passes the magnetism to the second coil. The voltage that leaves the transformer will be higher if there are more turns on the second coil.

Thick wires

It is cheaper to carry electricity a long way over thick wires. Less electricity is lost as heat because there is less resistance in the thick wires. The cables carried by pylons are made from thick steel wire.

Using electricity

Electricity has many advantages. It is easily changed into heat. Electricity is clean. It is easy to control. This is why many people think of electricity as the ideal source of energy. Since 1920, the demand for electricity has doubled every ten years.

At home

We use electricity in many different ways at home. Electric motors make machines turn. This works the blades of electric lawnmowers and turns a record player.

We use electricity to keep warm in winter and to heat water. Also, electricity helps us to keep cool in summer. It works fans and air conditioning systems as well as the motors used in refrigerators and deep freezers.

Electricity makes light in light bulbs and makes pictures appear on television and computer screens. Calculators and computers can solve difficult problems very quickly using electricity. Electricity runs clocks and it can switch machines on and off at set times. Even the door bell uses electricity.

▼ Most kitchens are full of things that use electricity.

light

telephone

microwave

washing machine

radio

cooker

toaster   coffee maker

food mixer

knife

blender

iron

refrigerator

oven

At work

Some people travel to work by electric train. Underground trains, escalators and lifts use electricity too. People use electricity at work as well as at home. Electric motors work many of the machines in factories. Electricity makes heat to melt steel. It lights and heats factories. Even when other fuels are used, such as gas and oil, electricity controls the heat with switches and pumps.

Farmers also depend on electricity. If there is a power cut, a dairy farmer may have to milk 100 cows by hand. Hay driers and greenhouses are heated by electricity. Electricity controls machines that water crops and feed animals. Today, it is difficult for us to imagine a world without electricity.

▼ In many factories, the work is done by electrical machines. These robots are making cars. Robots are automatic. They work without the help of people.

Keeping energy safe

▼ The waste from nuclear power stations is very small but it is very dangerous. The danger can last for thousands of years. Trains carrying nuclear waste are kept away from other traffic. The waste is put into special strong containers, like the third wagon from the front on this train.

Many people take risks to supply us with energy. If a mine floods or a roof collapses, coal miners may die. Some mining disasters are caused by gas explosions. Oil and gas workers face dangers from fire and explosions, storms and accidents.

People are sometimes hurt or killed at home because of suffocation from fumes, gas explosions, or **electric shocks**. Electricity can flow through your body if you touch live wires. A low voltage might give you an electric shock. A high voltage will burn you or kill you.

Electricity

Great care is taken to make electricity safe. Machines and circuits have fuses to stop them getting too hot. Live wires are **insulated**. This means they are covered with plastic and other materials that have a high resistance to electricity. Electricity cannot flow through these materials. They stop fingers touching live wires by accident. Electrical machines should all be **earthed**. In an emergency, a special wire carries electricity from the machine to a plate or pipe outside the house. This means that if a fault occurs, the electricity goes safely to the ground.

Gas and oil

Natural gas is not poisonous but it can be dangerous. It catches fire very easily. An explosion is always possible if there is a gas leak. People could suffocate if there are no open windows through which the gas can escape. A smell is added to natural gas so people know if there is a leak.

The greatest risk with oil is pollution. If a tanker or a pipeline is damaged, leaking oil kills wildlife. When an oil tanker delivers oil to a refinery, the ships' tanks have to be cleaned. Captains of oil tankers are not allowed to empty the dirty water back into the sea.

Nuclear power

There is a possible danger of **radiation** from nuclear power stations. An accident could send streams of particles from nuclear fuel into the air. We cannot see, taste or feel radiation. Radiation carries energy but a large amount can be harmful. It can make people ill and it can kill them. The workers at nuclear power stations take great care to prevent leaks. Accidents are rare. The worst was at the Russian nuclear power plant at Chernobyl in 1986. It affected many other countries besides the USSR because the wind blew the radiation over those countries that are next to the USSR. It will be many years before scientists can tell just how much damage was done.

▼ A fire on the oil tanker *Atlantic Empress* burned for many days.

Running out of energy

The amount of energy which people use each day depends on the way they live. Long ago, when people lived in caves, they had only wood fires to keep them warm or to cook on. Later, people used animals to help them with their work. In many parts of the world, people's lives began to change about 150 years ago. This was when coal was first used to power factories and trains. Finding oil led to even bigger changes. Oil was cheap and easy to carry to different parts of the world. Oil made life easier for about one-quarter of the people in the world. Better ways were found to move coal and natural gas too.

Is there enough of this energy for everyone in the world? Today, we are using up fossil fuels very quickly because they are so useful. These fossil fuels will not last forever.

▼ The larger pictures show the amount of each fossil fuel left in the world. The smaller pictures show how much is used up each year. People think there is enough coal for another 300 years. Gas may last 60 years but oil may only last about 35 years.

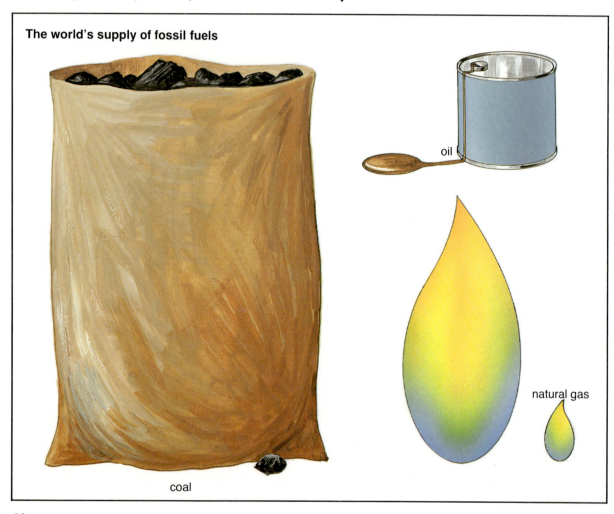

The world's supply of fossil fuels

oil

natural gas

coal

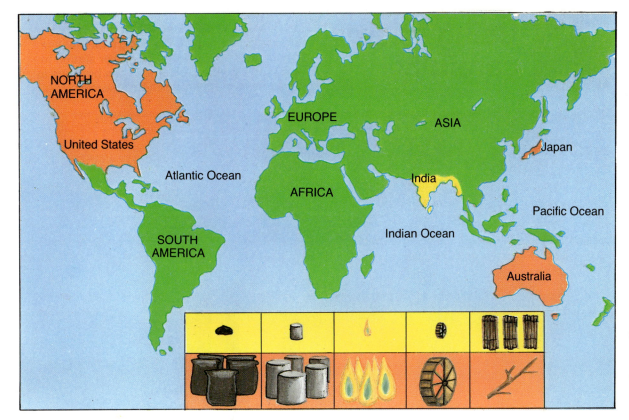

Oil crisis

One-quarter of the people in the world own two-thirds of the fossil fuels. Many countries do not have enough money to buy fossil fuels from the owners. Richer countries buy from people who have more fossil fuels than they use. When energy is cheap, people use as much as they want. They may even waste it.

In 1973, a group of oil-producing countries got together. They decided to put up the price of their oil. Suddenly, oil was not cheap any more. It cost four times as much. Even the United States and Western Europe could not afford to buy so much oil. Motorists had to queue for petrol. Factories made fewer goods. People realized how much they needed oil. They began to insulate their homes. This made it possible for them to heat their homes with less oil. People bought smaller cars which used less petrol.

▲ Some people use a lot more energy each year than others. Nearly one-third of all the world's energy is used in the United States. Far more people live in India than in the United States. The people of India only use a tiny amount of the world's energy.

Fuel in the future

Some experts think people will discover new oil and gasfields. Running out of fuel may not be a problem after all. Burning fossil fuels is a problem though. It adds gases to the air. In some places, this pollution is making trees die. It may also be changing the world's weather. Many people would like to see more use made of renewable energy, such as the Sun, wind, running water, waves and tides. They want to make sure the world is still a pleasant place to live in the future. Protecting the world and the useful things in it is called **conservation**.

Using energy carefully

▼ This type of power station wastes huge amounts of energy. A chemical heat pipeline could carry energy from the power station to where it is needed. Electricity can be made in small generators near people's homes.

Some people search all day for wood to cook a meal. They carry heavy bundles a long way. They do not waste the fuel. There could be enough energy in the world for everyone to live in comfort. The problem is how to make sure everyone has a fair share of the energy. Energy is not spread evenly all over the world. Taking oil, gas or coal from distant places costs a lot of money. People who live far away from big cities cannot always pay for a pipeline or a tanker to deliver oil, gas or coal. We have to find the best ways to carry energy to everyone. Energy could be cheaper for everyone if we used less, and none was wasted.

Using waste

A lot of heat is wasted when fossil fuels burn. Insulating a house keeps heat in and saves energy. Factories send heat from their machines into the air through chimneys. Power stations lose huge amounts of energy as heat when they make electricity. This heat could be used to heat buildings. At the moment, it is difficult to collect this heat and carry it very far. In some places waste heat is piped as hot gas to buildings nearby. Cars push heat out through their exhausts. Machines called **heat exchangers** can use heat from an engine to heat the inside of a car, bus or train.

Less waste

A lot of energy is used to make paper, boxes and cans that we buy things in. These wrappers are just thrown away. We do not need to make so many. More energy is used to carry rubbish away. Sometimes the rubbish is just buried. Glass bottles, metal cans and paper can be used to make new, or **recycled**, things. Waste can also be used as a source of more energy. When huge amounts of rubbish are burned, there is enough heat given off to make electricity.

◄ Saving energy by turning off lights is one way to make the world's sources of energy last longer. Posters like this help to remind people that they can do something to help.

▼ In the future, many more homes will be built like this. They will be just as warm and as convenient as homes are today. They will be much cheaper to heat and light. When less energy is used, less energy has to be carried around the world.

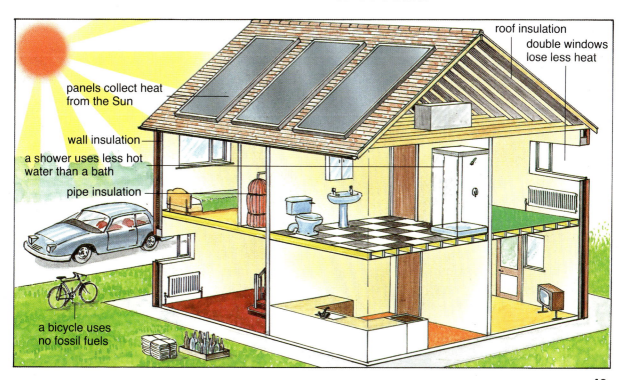

roof insulation

double windows lose less heat

panels collect heat from the Sun

wall insulation

a shower uses less hot water than a bath

pipe insulation

a bicycle uses no fossil fuels

Energy and the future

▼ Scientists are always looking for new ways to carry energy. One idea is to build special roads over the Arctic ice.

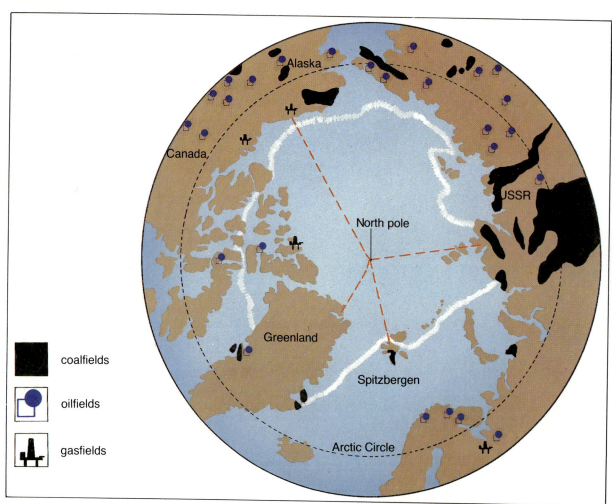

- ■ coalfields
- ● oilfields
- ⊥ gasfields

The best source of energy would be safe, cheap and easy to use. It would power vehicles as well as provide heat for power stations. It would not spoil the air or the earth in any way. It would also be renewable. At the moment, we do not have one fuel or source of energy like this. They all have faults. The non-renewable sources of energy, such as coal, oil and gas sometimes pollute the land, the air and the seas and rivers.

Wind, water and Sun

Many of the renewable sources of energy, such as the winds, waves, tides and the Sun, are still too expensive to provide whole cities with energy. They are not as easy to use in power stations as fossil fuels. They are already useful enough to supply small amounts of energy. Most people who use renewable energy live next to their windmill or have solar panels on the roof of their home. In the future it may be possible to carry renewable energy over longer distances.

Wind power already produces electricity in parts of California. The main drawback is the fact that 300 large and noisy windmills are needed to take the place of just one coal-burning power station.

Collecting electricity

Heat from the Sun can also be used as a source of energy but energy is often needed when the Sun is not shining. Buildings need lights at night. More heat is needed in the winter when the Sun does not shine so often. Scientists are trying to find better ways of storing the Sun's energy for future use. Energy from the Sun could be very useful because the Sun shines all over the world. The energy does not have to be carried from one place to another.

New ideas

The head of an American oil company wants to build a highway across the North Pole. He thinks the road could be built at a low cost from a new form of ice. When water is sprayed into very cold air, it freezes into tiny pieces. This ice is very strong and could be used to make the road. There are huge oilfields under the Arctic ice. Oil could be carried to the United States, the USSR and northern Europe along this polar road. A city could grow up near the North Pole. It could use a new source of energy because the Earth's magnetism is very powerful at the pole.

When heat can be sent by pipeline there is no need to carry a source of energy. In New Mexico in the United States, gas is heated by solar power. The hot gas is piped to buildings where it is used for heating or to make electricity. The cool gas then returns to be heated and used again. Heat from deep under the ground and waste heat from power stations could be piped in the same way. Buildings would not need mains electricity or gas supplies or need to store oil or coal for central heating systems or fires.

▼ Engineers are thinking of building power stations out at sea. They could take gas directly from a gasfield and turn it into electricity. They would not need to transport it first in tankers or through long pipelines.

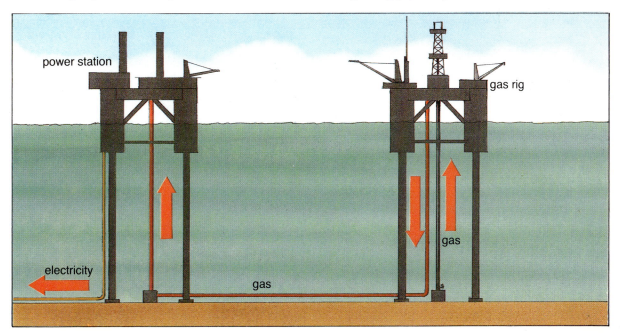

Glossary

acid: a strong substance which can eat away solid things, such as metals

atom: the smallest part of a substance

bulk carrier: a large ship which carries a loose dry cargo, like grain

cable: a thick rope made of wires. Cables used for carrying electricity are protected by a thick plastic outer covering

carbon: an important substance found in fossil fuels and all living things

catalyst: a substance which helps a chemical reaction to take place, but does not change itself

chemical energy: a type of energy made when two or more substances mix

chemical reaction: the change which happens when one substance is joined or mixed with another substance

circuit: the complete path of an electric current. If the circuit is broken, the current will not flow

compass: an instrument used to find direction. It contains a needle which points north

conservation: the protection and careful use of something. The protection of the countryside, wildlife, or an old building is called conservation

conveyor belt: a very long strip or belt of strong material which is moved over rollers by a motor. Things put on the flat surface are carried along

crude oil: oil which is still in the same state as it was when it came out of the ground

diesel: a type of engine that burns heavy oil. The diesel engine was invented by Rudolph Diesel

earth: to direct electricity into the ground

electric current: a flow of electricity

electricity: a kind of energy or power which can travel along wires. It is used to heat and light homes, run factories and work many machines

electric shock: the tingling or burning feeling experienced when someone touches something that has an electric current running through it

electromagnet: an iron bar with a coil of wire around it. The iron bar acts like a magnet when an electric current is passed through it

electron: a tiny particle of electricity which is found in all atoms. It carries a negative charge

energy: the power to do work. People get energy from food. Engines get energy from fuel

energy cycle: the change from heat or work energy to stored energy and from stored energy back to heat or work energy

evaporate: to change from a liquid into a gas

filament: a very fine thread, usually of wire. The filament in an electric light bulb is made from a wire with a high melting point. It glows white hot when an electric current passes through it

fluorescent light: a bright light made by ultraviolet rays in a special tube

fossil fuel: a material which can be burned that comes from the remains of animals and plants that lived millions of years ago. Coal and oil are fossil fuels

fraction: a part of something. Part of a liquid mixture, such as crude oil

fractionating tower: a tall tube used in processing crude oil. Different products are collected at each level

freight: goods carried by any form of transport such as planes, ships or trucks

fuel: a material which burns. Fuel burned in engines makes power for movement

fuse: a safety device made of thin wire which melts if an appliance gets overheated

gas plant: a place where natural gas is treated by adding a smell so it can be detected

generate: to make or create electricity

geothermal power: the heat in hot water springs and geysers. They are heated by the molten rock inside the Earth

grid: a set of straight lines or wires which cross each other to make pattern of square shapes. A grid is used on maps

heat exchanger: a device for passing heat from one liquid to another without the liquids mixing

hopper house: a building with large funnel-shaped storage chambers. The material to be stored is poured in at the top and let out in smaller quantities through a narrow base

hydrocarbon: a mixture of chemicals which includes carbon and hydrogen

hydro-electricity: electricity which has been made by using the power of fast-flowing water to drive a turbine

hydrogen: a gas which is very light and burns easily

insulate: (1) to stop electricity from passing through or along something. (2) to prevent heat from being lost

kinetic energy: the energy in something when it moves

magnet: a piece of metal that attracts objects made of iron or steel towards it, or forces them away

magnetism: having the power to attract

mechanical energy: energy made by a machine, or in a way that is similar to that of a machine

meter: an instrument or device which measures or counts

molecule: the smallest part of a mixture of chemicals. A molecule is made up at least two atoms

negative charge: the electrical charge carried by an electron. It has the opposite force to a positive charge

neutron: a tiny particle at the centre of an atom. It does not carry an electrical charge

non-renewable: something which cannot be replaced or renewed when it is used up

nuclear power station: a place where energy is produced by splitting atoms

nucleus: the centre of an atom. It is made of electrically charged protons and neutrons

petrol: a liquid made from crude oil. It burns very easily and is used as a fuel in car engines

pole: either of the two ends of a magnet

pollution: something which dirties or poisons the air, land or water, such as waste chemicals from factories

positive charge: an electrical charge carried by a proton. It has the opposite force to a negative charge

potential energy: stored energy which can be used

proton: a tiny particle of electricity which is found at the centre of all atoms. It carries a positive charge

pylon: a tall, steel frame for supporting electricity cables above the ground

radiant energy: a type of energy that is given out in waves, or radiated, from a particular place like a fire or the Sun

radiation: rays from the centre of an atom which is splitting up. These rays are dangerous to living things

recycling: using waste material again. Recycling can help to save energy

refinery: a place where a raw material is made pure. Oil is refined into petrol, diesel oil and other products in a refinery

renewable: something which can be replaced or put back after being used

resistance: the extent to which something can slow down movement. Thin copper wire can slow down the flow of electricity more than thick copper wire

single buoy mooring: a place set up for supertankers to stop at. The mooring is in deep water off the coast and linked to the land by a pipeline

slurry: a mixture of a solid, such as crushed rock, with water. Slurry can be transported by a pipeline because it is a liquid

static electricity: an electric charge produced by rubbing

tanker: a ship built to carry large amounts of liquids

transformer: a machine which increases or decreases the force of an electric current

tungsten: a heavy metal with a very high melting point. It can be made into a very fine wire and is used in electric light bulbs

turbine: a wheel which has many curved blades. It is spun around rapidly by the movement of a gas or a liquid. Turbines drive machines which make electricity

vacuum: an empty space with no air or any other matter in it

voltage: a measurement of the force of an electric current

weighbridge: a large weighing machine built into a road. It is used for measuring the weight of the load on a truck

Index